my cold plum lemon pie bluesy mood

by **Tameka Fryer Brown**

illustrated by

Shane W. Evans

Viking

An Imprint of Penguin Group (USA) Inc.

Viking

Published by the Penguin Group

Penguin Young Readers Group, 345 Hudson Street, New York, New York 10014, U.S.A.

Penguin Group (Canada), 90 Eglinton Avenue East, Suite 700, Toronto, Ontario, Canada M4P 2Y3 (a division of Pearson Penguin Canada Inc.)

Penguin Books Ltd, 80 Strand, London WC2R 0RL, England

Penguin Ireland, 25 St Stephen's Green, Dublin 2, Ireland (a division of Penguin Books Ltd)

Penguin Group (Australia), 250 Camberwell Road, Camberwell, Victoria 3124, Australia (a division of Pearson Australia Group Pty Ltd)

Penguin Books India Pvt Ltd, 11 Community Centre, Panchsheel Park, New Delhi – 110 017, India

Penguin Group (NZ), 67 Apollo Drive, Rosedale, Auckland 0632, New Zealand (a division of Pearson New Zealand Ltd.)

Penguin Books (South Africa) (Pty) Ltd, 24 Sturdee Avenue, Rosebank, Johannesburg 2196, South Africa

Penguin Books Ltd, Registered Offices: 80 Strand, London WC2R 0RL, England

First published in the United States of America by Viking, a division of Penguin Young Readers Group, 2013

1 3 5 7 9 10 8 6 4 2

Text copyright © Tameka Brown, 2013
Illustrations copyright © Shane Evans, 2013
All rights reserved

LIBRARY OF CONGRESS CATALOGING-IN-PUBLICATION DATA

Brown, Tameka Fryer.
My cold plum lemon pie bluesy mood / by Tameka Fryer Brown ; illustrated by Shane Evans.
p. cm.
Summary: Jamie describes his mood throughout the day, using colors and rhythmic text, as he changes from an "easy green mood"
while drawing a picture for his sister to a "brooding black mood" when he is teased for doing so.
ISBN 978-0-670-01285-5 (hardcover)
[1. Stories in rhyme. 2. Mood (Psychology)—Fiction. 3. African Americans—Fiction.] I. Evans, Shane, ill. II. Title.
PZ8.3.B8157Col 2013   [E]—dc23   2012016781

Manufactured in China
Set in Linoletter
This art is digital collage created with oil paints and graphite.

ALWAYS LEARNING   PEARSON

For Noah Jamal, because you are loved. —T. F. B.

Thank you GOD . . . This MOOD is dedicated to my GRANDMA . . .
she is the reason I know the colors of JOY and LOVE. —S. W. E.

I'm in a mood
A feeling kind of mood
A being kind of mood
Is what I'm in

A **purple** kind of mood
Cold-plum eating
Grape-juice drinking
On the couch
Bobbing to the beat kind of mood
A purple kind of mood
That's what I'm in

Now I'm headed
To a **gray** kind of place
Storm brewing inside
That I hide
'Cause I don't want any trouble space
Dark and swelling
Looming
Gloomy gray kind of place
That's what I'm in

Slowly

I ease

Into gentle **green**

A dragon dancing . . .

In the jungle . . .

On some Jell-O green

Little sis smiling really
  wide green

Even let her kiss my cheek

Easy green mood

That's what I'm in

MAD!
So mad my
Mood turns **black**
Black hole inside screams
Take it back!
But I swallow that . . .
STOP

No more hugs
Brooding black mood
That's what I'm in

Bomp, bomp
Bip, bip, bap
Orange mood
Moving, schooling
To the hoop
Swish!
J in your face, doin'
  what I do
Swish!
Fake left, slide right
Swish! and *swish!*
Sweet orange mood
That's what I'm in

RED!

RUN!

Gotta get home!
Fire-engine-roaring-down-
  the-street-hot-flames-
  shooting-from-my-feet-
  don't-stop-to-take-a-
  breath-till-I-make-it-
  through-the-door *RED!*

Whew!

Raced the dark and made
  it in

Shake me, shove me
Into **brown**
This time
I won't be pushed
   around!
Planted . . . fierce . . .
Not backing down—
GRRRRRRR!
Big, strong brown
I win!

Rowdy, hungry
Yellow mood
Dinner—full of *payday* food!
Baked corn pudding
Bless this meal . . .

Curry chicken
That's my piece!
Loud talk, laughter
Lemon pie
Lively yellow mood
That's what we're in

That's okay—
Cool, **blue** okay
Time with myself
In my own space
Hands swirling 'round
In liquid peace
Sailing on waves
In the sky of my mind
A bluesy kind of mood
That's what I'm in

Yeah, I'm in a mood
A feeling kind of mood
A being kind of mood
Is what I'm in . . .

A living, breathing
Cold-plum eating
Being kind of mood

That's what I'm in.